The Magic Porridge Pot

Based on a story by the Brothers Grimm

Retold by Rosie Dickins

Illust ... ordon

H annah had little money...

and even less food.

Sigh!

But whatever
she had, she
always shared.

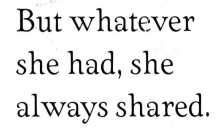

One day, Hannah was
out for a walk when
she saw some bees.

"Aha!" she thought.
"Bees mean honey."

As Hannah ate the honey,
an old woman hobbled up,
swinging an empty pot.

"Would you like some honey?" asked Hannah.

"Ooh, yes please!" said the woman.

"It will go perfectly with my porridge."

"Porridge? What porridge?" said Hannah.

The woman smiled.
"Watch!" she said.

Cook pot, cook!

With a sizzle of magic,
steaming porridge
filled the pot.

Stop pot, stop!

Then, just as quickly,
it stopped.

They each ate a bowl of delicious porridge
drizzled with sweet, sticky honey.

"Would you like the pot?" said the woman.
"Remember the magic words and
you'll never go hungry again."

Mmmm!

Mmmm!

From then on, Hannah had plenty to eat.

She had porridge for breakfast...

porridge for lunch...

...and porridge for supper.

One evening, a greedy boy
smelled the porridge.

Mmm, what's that?

He followed his nose
to Hannah's cottage.

He saw the pot start to fill with porridge...

...but Hannah drew the curtains, so he didn't see it stop.

The boy waited for
Hannah to go to bed.

Then he tiptoed in,

grabbed the pot...

...and ran all
the way home.

He couldn't wait to shout the magic words.

Cook pot, cook!

CAT

With a sizzle of magic,
the pot filled with porridge.

It got fuller...

and fuller...

"That's enough," said the boy.
"You can stop now."

But the pot didn't stop.

Puddles of porridge
poured onto the floor.

"That's too much," cried the boy. "Stop, I tell you!"

Uh-oh...

But the pot didn't stop.

It filled the room
with a gloopy sea
of porridge.

Soon, porridge was
pouring out of the
doors and windows.

"Please stop!"
begged the boy.

But the pot didn't stop.

The boy sploshed
out into the night.

Help!

"Stop, stop, STOP!" he yelled.
"I'll drown in porridge!"

But still the pot didn't stop.

In her bedroom,
Hannah sniffed.

"That smells like porridge!"
she thought.

She raced outside.
Porridge was flooding
down the street.

Oh no! It must be the pot.

Hannah shouted
the magic words.

Stop pot, stop!

And, at last, the pot stopped.
The greedy boy was saved.

He couldn't return
Hannah's pot fast enough.
And he never stole
anything again.

Designed by Caroline Spatz
Edited by Jenny Tyler and Lesley Sims

This edition first published in 2012 by Usborne Publishing Ltd.,
Usborne House, 83-85 Saffron Hill, London EC1N 8RT, England. www.usborne.com
Copyright © 2012, 2010 Usborne Publishing Ltd.